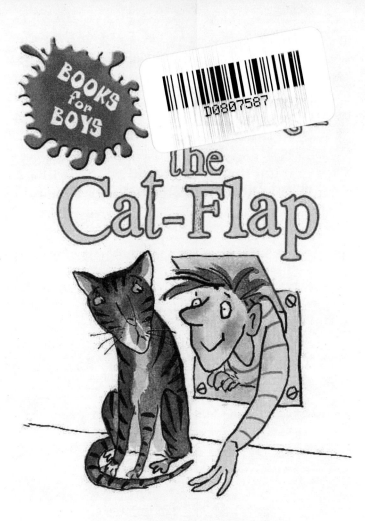

the Cat-Flap

BOOKS for BOYS

IAN WHYBROW
ILLUSTRATED BY **TONY ROSS**

Hodder
Children's
Books

a division of Hachette Children's Books

Many thanks to the Russell family in Paddington, Sydney and especially to Julian, who had the wonderful idea of sending his twins Tahlia and Remy on a key-hunt through the cat-flap in his house.

With grateful thanks to Jo and all the brilliant staff and children at Megan Baker House, Moreton Eye, Leominster, Herefordshire.

Text copyright © 2006 Ian Whybrow
Illustrations copyright © 2006 Tony Ross
First published in Great Britain in 2006
by Hodder Children's Books

13

A Catalogue record for this book is available
from the British Library

ISBN: 978 0 340 911129

Printed and bound in Great Britain by
Clays Ltd, St Ives plc

The paper and board used in this paperback by
Hodder Children's Books are natural recyclable products made from
wood grown in sustainable forests. The manufacturing processes conform
to the environmental regulations of the country of origin.

Hodder Children's Books
a division of Hachette Children's Books
338 Euston Road, London NW1 3BH
An Hachette UK Company
www.hachette.co.uk

1

Thinking Out Loud

I'm Thomas Leo Falling. I live at Well Cottage, Overton, Herefordshire and I'm trying to think of the best place to start this story. Yes, I *know* where you're supposed to start. With the start!

But where *is* the start? The cat-flap? My legs? My twin sisters? Mum nearly getting arrested? Help!

I'll do Miss Suggs for you. She's my teacher at Rowan Primary.

Ready? (Loud squeaky voice.)
"Think about the setting and the
characters, Thomas. Start at the
beginning and keep it simple."

Well, tough! This is my story and
it's complicated.
I'm starting
with the vase.
Come into the
kitchen. You'll
have to go a
bit slowly
because I
can't walk
fast. I fall
over a lot
because I'm like
my name, Falling. I tell my legs
where to move but they don't do

what I tell them. Don't worry, I'm used to hitting the ground. Anyway, I'm all right if I've got something to hang on to. So how old do you think I am?

WHAT DO YOU MEAN, TWO AND A HALF!!!!! Don't be a turnip! I'm nearly ten, so watch it!

Where are we? In the kitchen. Right, come over here. See the door to the cupboard under the sink? Open it. Phew – what a pong! Don't worry. It's just because of the leak in the waste-pipe. My dad's stopped fixing things because …

Wait a minute! This is not the part where I tell you about my family. This is the part where I tell you about the vase.

Now. We're sitting on the floor. This is a good position to see things from. We're looking in the cupboard under the sink. Can you see the washing-up liquid? See the bleach? See the paper sack of dry cat food gone soggy because of the leak? Now look behind. I don't mean the bendy pipe. I mean BEHIND the bendy pipe. See that tall china thing?

Good. That's it! That's the vase.

It's about fifty centimetres tall.
Have you done cylinders at school?
OK, then it's like a china cylinder.
Only it spreads out at the top. It's
painted red, green, yellow and
purply-blue. How do I know all
this? Because I've looked at it tons
of times. I like it.

If you look closely, you can see
this king sitting on a throne. There
are people kneeling and bowing
down, banging their heads on the
floor. I don't know what all the
trees and rocks are doing near a
throne, but that's vases for you.

Here's a secret. This vase is
worth a *fortune*. What a shame if it
got SMASHED.

Dad's Dark Time

Right, now it's time to say about my family. I think I'll do Dad first. That's because the story I'm going to tell you happened a little while ago when Dad got stuck. I call that time Dad's Dark Time.

So here we go. My dad is Duncan Falling the poet. His Dark Time was last year when he just stopped saying anything. Mum said he was *depressed*. I like *stuck* better.

It was like the word part of his brain got stuck on hold. Can you believe, it was nearly six months and not one word came, not one poem? It was horrible. Not just for him, for all of us. Normally he's funny and nice and he can fix anything. All the time he was stuck, he just wanted to lie in bed or go out and drink too much beer.

He's quite tall with long scruffy hair (but nice) and he's skinny, like me. He's got a scar right across his cheek and chin because he used to climb mountains. When he was 17, he could climb right round the room WITHOUT TOUCHING THE FLOOR. How? By just holding on to the picture rail! Oh, and after that he was a hippy or a gypsy, I forget which. That's when he had all his other wives and eleven children. They're *years* older than me and the twins. That's enough about them. Back to my dad.

Dad is quite old but handsome and he likes black clothes. Normally he sings all the time. Even on the lav. The only part of his clothes that's not black is his glasses. They have green frames. He gets in the papers sometimes. Sometimes it's people writing about how brilliant his poems are. But in the Dark Time, he got in the papers by drinking beer.

Mum's got scrapbooks full of news about him. Here's something from the Dark Time:

The papers liked saying jokes about his name. They said it was Drunken instead of Duncan. The *Sun* called him **Drunk'n**

Duncan Disorderly!"

Falling Over. Ha ha, very funny, I don't think.

OK, he did get drunk a lot, but he's a poet and he had a lot of worries.

Busy Busy

My mum is lovely. She's thirty years younger than Dad and very pretty. She loves books and Latin and Greek but not beer. She was teaching Latin and Greek in a posh school when she met Dad and they fell in love and had me. Later, they had the twins, Gemma and Lottie. So Mum was too busy to carry on working in a school.

I made her busy because I came

out too soon. A small bit of blood bled into the walking part of my brain. That's all it took. They did loads of tests on me and the doctor said I would never walk. That was Mum's Dark Time but she put it behind her. She told me: "It was just bad luck. Bad things happen, but you put them behind you. You move on. You make good things happen."

Still, I was hard work for her, I guess. She had to help me more than most kids.

She taught me a lot. (And Dad.

He taught me all sorts.) So when I went to school, I was WAY ahead in reading, writing, music and sums and everything. I knew nearly all the Bob Dylan songs by heart. And The Rolling Stones. Also, I could say more Greek than my friend Dougie Christou, and he's a *Greek* person!! But I still couldn't move about much by myself, only in a wheelchair.

Then Mum heard of this special place. It's called Megan Baker House. Have you heard of it? It's like school, only not so many people in your class. You just go there for short visits two or three times a week. They don't have teachers; they have *conductors*. Becky, she was my conductor.

And Simon. They show you how to help yourself by using muscles you didn't even know you had.

When I first started there, I could just about crawl. But four weeks later, I could lift myself up, even do a couple of steps by myself! That time Mum and Dad came to collect me and I walked right over to them! I can't describe it. We were laughing

and crying at the same time! Do you know what wonderful means? Full of wonder. That's how we were.

I still have to use my wheelchair a lot, but you should see me walking now. Yes, I have to use sticks, but now we all say NUTS to that doctor who said I would never walk.

So how come my mum is *still* busy all the time? Don't tell me you forgot about Gemma and Lottie! They're enough to wear *anybody* out.

I think Dad was a bit worried when they were in Mum's tummy. In case they were unlucky getting born, like me. But when they came out safe, he was over the moon.

This is the poem he wrote for them.

Gemini

My Joy! My Gems! My Gemini!
I am in Heaven now and you are why.
Without the pair of you, I would have been
Unluckily, the father of thirteen!

Are You a Twin?

Gemini. That's Latin for twins in case you were wondering. Hey, maybe you could be a twin! Is your birthday between May 21st and June 20th? Yes? Then your star sign is Gemini.

My star sign is *Leo* and it's my middle name. It means lion. GRRRAAAAAH!

Do you know any twins aged eighteen months? I'm telling you,

Gemma and Lottie can drive you
NUTS! They run about, they shout,
they squabble. They don't talk
normal English.
They just talk
nonsense, like a
nursery rhyme
language.

For example,
Gemma sings,

"Arthur found a
tuppenny mice.
Arthur found a
tweakle, Dattsa
way your
mummy goes ..."

Then Lottie answers, "Pock! go da weagle!"

Then they both fall over on purpose.

That's why Mum was worn out. That's why she didn't have time to teach people Latin and Greek. So when Dad stopped writing his poems and fixing things, we had NO money. All we had was TROUBLE.

Mum's a double Gemini. Her name is June, because she was born on June 1st, under the sign of Gemini. AND she's got a twin sister, my Aunt Juniper. They look exactly the same. Exactly. They have long legs and feet, and they can both sit on their hair. Aunt Juniper's clever, like Mum, only she studied Art and

became a Professor. She's an expert on Chinese pots and plates and she was the one who gave Mum and Dad the vase I told you about.

So what was it doing in the cupboard under the sink? I thought you'd ask that.

OK, I'll keep it short. Mum fell in love with Dad, right? Aunt Juniper couldn't stand him. She said he was

miles too old and ugly for Mum.
"He's got too many wives and
children already," she wrote.
"Keep away! He is mad, bad and
dangerous. He will only make you
unhappy." Dad found the letter and
got angry. He wouldn't invite her to
the wedding, which was a proper
one with a cake and everything.
He wouldn't talk to her, even on
the phone. He wouldn't have her
near the house, not even to see me
after I was born. And then she went
off on her travels so I never even
saw her.

Not till a couple of weeks ago.

The Peace Offering

Aunt Juniper turned out to be
wrong. Dad didn't make Mum
unhappy. They got on brilliantly, we
all did. We were always laughing
and hugging and singing and
mucking around together – until
Dad's Dark Time started. It started
just after Mum's birthday last year.
It was so BAD, I thought it would
never end.

Mum's birthday was a big one,

her thirtieth. That's why Aunt Juniper
sent the vase. She was living in
China and she sent it from Shanghai
in a special box.

Dad was scribbling something in
his notebook when
the parcel arrived.
"What do you think,
Dunk?" Mum said,
taking the vase out
and holding it up to
the light.

Dad carried on scribbling.
He's like that when he's
got an idea.

"It's from Juniper."

Dad looked up. He put down his
pencil. His face started changing
colour.

24

"Isn't it lovely?" smiled Mum, turning it to look at the pictures. "I think it's for all of us – a peace offering. It says on the card: *With special love to all of you. I miss you so much.*"

Dad's face was blazing red. He opened his mouth. He tried to say something. Nothing came out. He tried again. Nothing. So he got up, left the room and banged the door behind him.

Mum said quietly,

"I don't think your dad's quite ready to make peace with Juniper yet. I think we'd better hide the vase away until we can think of a way to get them to be friends. It's such a fragile thing. I'd hate to see it get broken."

So we put it in a place where we thought Dad would NEVER look. You know where.

It stayed in that cupboard for six months, tucked away, a bit like Aunt Juniper was. But now and then, when Dad was down the pub getting drunk, Mum and I would take it out and gaze at it. The twins would be in bed so it was just the two of us. "Look at the colours on it!" Mum would say.

"It's fantastaculous!" I'd say. That used to make her laugh. "Is it worth a lot?" I'd ask.

"Might be," she'd say. "One day I'll get it valued. But it's precious to me even if it's only  worth 50p, because Juniper sent it. It's about all I've got left of her, apart from Christmas and birthday cards."

"Don't worry," I'd say. "I bet you ANYTHING, she'll just … turn up one day. Then we'll MAKE her and Dad like each other, eh?"

Mum hates crying but she couldn't stop a tear from sneaking out.

"Piggies might fly," she said.

Incognito

The day Mum nearly got arrested
(I think it was December 17th) Dad
actually got out of bed and helped
Mum put my wheelchair in the back
of the car. For December it wasn't
that cold and the sun was really
bright. Maybe that was why. He
even agreed to look after the twins
while Mum drove me to school.
He still wasn't SAYING anything,
and wasn't happy about it because

you could tell he had a headache, but he agreed.

We had this Morris Minor Estate, the one with the wooden doors at the back. Not many cars get wood-worm, but ours did. The engine was brilliant but there was a fair bit of rust that we really needed Dad to sort out. From where I sat, you could see the road through the floor if you moved the mat.

We had a nice ride through the woods and along the lanes to school.

We could hear something going clinketty clink under one of the wheels, but we weren't bothered.

"Must have run over a bit of chicken wire or something," said Mum. We sang "Like a Rolling Stone" really loud, so we forgot about the other noise for a while.

Anyway, when we got to school, there was a policeman there, checking cars. He came over to us while Mum was getting out my wheelchair. "Oh, dear," he said, looking at the back tyre. "Oh dear, oh dear, oh dear!"

Mum said, "Don't worry, it's only a bit of chicken wire."

He said, "That's not chicken wire. You've worn away so much

rubber, you're down to the wire underneath! That is not just illegal, that is DANGEROUS. I could arrest you for that, Ma'am."

Mum said, "Really? You're not proposing to lock me up, are you, officer? I am a mother of three!"

He said, "I'm just going to give you a warning this time, Ma'am. But if I catch you driving this car in the condition AGAIN …" He closed his eyes and shook his head.

He must have been thinking of the dark, damp cell down at the station.

When Mum came to fetch me home, she was wearing dark glasses and a ginger wig. "Any sign of that policeman?" she hissed as she bundled me into the back of the car.

"No," I said. "Mum, why are you wearing that ...?"

"Good," she whispered. "But better safe than sorry. If that policeman recognizes me, we're all done for! But he'll never spot me if I'm *incognito*."

I guessed that must be Latin for *in disguise*.

I knew she hadn't changed the tyre because she didn't have the money, simple as that.

Slam!

Next day was Saturday, so no school. The twins were running about in their duffel coats and tutus. They had their arms out being fairies or bluebottles or something.

"Wee Willy Wonka went inna train," sang Gemma.

"Upstair, down a stair, inna night AGAIN!" sang Lottie. They kept bumping into things but that didn't stop them.

"Can't you read to them or something, Tom?" Mum said. I said no way. It would be like standing in the middle of the motorway trying to read to the traffic.

Mum and Dad had this old chest of drawers in the kitchen. They'd tipped all the clothes out of it and were giving it a bit of a polish.

Dad was grumpy about it, but at least he was doing something and that was a good sign.

It was Mum's idea to sell it. She said it was worth a couple of hundred at least and she knows this bloke, Lemon they call him because of the look on his face. He's got a shop in the village. It's called Lane Antiques, sells all sorts of junk.

Dad made a noise. More like a groan, really.

My heart stopped. Mum held her breath. Was he going to say something at last?

No. Nothing else. Not a dicky bird.

"Oh do shut up, Duncan," said Mum, pretending they were having an argument. "I know this chest belonged to your granddad. But we can't do without the car and we need new tyres. No choice."

Lottie and Gemma were getting over-excited. They'd started that "All Fall Down" thing. One of them lies flat out on the floor and the other one crashes on top.

After that, when it was time for Mum and Dad to load up the car, the twins wanted to go outside and "help". No choice again. Either they got to carry a little drawer to the car or they screamed your eardrums out.

I can't manage drawers and my sticks at the same time, so my job was holding the back doors open with my bum. The twins were in their tutus but at least they had their duffel coats on. I was still in my jim-jams and dressing gown. Oh, and a pullover, which was good because it was nippy out there!

Mum and Dad jumped in the car. They both had to go because it needed two people to unload the chest at the other end.

Mum wound down her window and waved to the twins: "You stay there with Thomas. You can watch CBeebies. Be good!

Won't be long," she called.

Lottie and Gemma said,
"Yayyyy!" Then they jumped up and
down going, "Cee bee, Marjory Dee!
Johnny can hab a new marker!"

The car turned the corner. I just
stopped for a second to shift a snail
off the path with my stick. And that's
when I heard the front door slam.

Locked Out

"Ha ha – BANG!" shouted Lottie, who was still hanging on to the brass handle under the letterbox.

Gemma ran up to her and smacked the door with both hands. She wanted to say *Ha ha BANG* too. They both said it about ten times.

"Oh well done, you've locked us out," I said in my most sarcastic voice. "Oh dear, no Ceebees."

"WHAAAA!" they wailed.

"EEEE!" they screamed.

My eardrums!

"Only kidding!" I said. It's not fair if you've got to use sticks. You can't stuff your fingers in your ears. "Come on – round the back."

"Wee Willy Wonka, Run rounda back!" they went, and shot round the corner.

By the time I'd staggered round to the back door, they were banging the glass panel. "Mind out," I said and reached past them to turn the doorknob. Uh-oh. The back door was locked as well.

"Flea bly mice!" Gemma said to Lottie, and Lottie agreed.

I looked up at the bedroom windows – but they were all shut, it being so chilly. Not that I could have got up there anyway.

"Pock! go da weagle," said Gemma to Lottie. Pop! In went their thumbs, into their mouths together. I'm telling you, they live in a world of their own.

I peered through the smeary handprints into the kitchen. I could see the breakfast things on the kitchen table. And on the far side of

the room – what was that, dangling from a hook on the dresser? The keys!

"Oh no! How the heck am I going to get those?" I moaned. Something whacked me on the bum. It was Gemma. She had a brick in her hand. So did Lottie.

"Flea four, Knock on da door!" they yelled. They were trying to get me out of the way so they could bash the glass in.

"No! No bashing!" I said.

At that moment, Henry, our cat appeared. As he jumped down off the garden wall, the twins saw him,

too. They took out their thumbs –
pop – and made little grabbing
movements with their fingers. "Mimi!"
they cried. "Ahhh, Mimi!"

Henry was nervous. They'd already
tried to squeeze him into a fairy
costume that morning. So he dived
out the way – through the cat-flap.

DING! I had an idea. "Through
there, Gemma!" I rattled the cat-flap
with my stick to show her. "In!
Gemma, in!"

"Nin nin nin," said Gemma
helpfully.

"That's it," I said. "Good girl!" She
got down on all fours and used her
head like a battering ram against the
funny little door. Soon she was in up
to her tutu. Then she got stuck.

"Hold on,"
I said. I sat
down and
gave her a
little push.
Bingo!
"Nah nah nah
nah!" she sang,
running to and
fro, enjoying her new freedom.
"Ooka me! Inna kitchy!"

"Gemma!" I called. "Gemma!"
She was way too excited to take
any notice. She went spinning
round and round, faster and faster.

"Gemma! Get Tommy the key!"
I called, but it was hopeless. She
was having too much fun getting
giddy. Whoops! she grabbed hold of

the leg of the table for support. Lucky, really, because Henry had his face in the milk jug. The table scraped across the stone floor.

"Miaow!" screeched Henry and shot out of the room. On the way, he knocked the jug over and Puffed Wheat sprayed everywhere.

"Mimi!" wailed Gemma and disappeared after the cat.

"Nooo!" I shouted. "Gemma! Come back! Please!"

"Gemma!" screamed Lottie. She pointed her finger at me as if I'd stolen her darling twin. "My Gemma! Gone!"

She made such a fuss I decided, OK, might as well push her through the cat-flap, too. In she went – SNAP. Great! Now maybe Lottie would get the keys.

"Girls," I wailed, banging on the glass. "Come back and bring Tommy the key!"

The twins ran back in. "Pee-bo!" they said, and ran out again, giggling.

"I'm not playing Pee-bo!" I shouted. "Come back in the kitchen!"

Nothing. Not a sound. "Mummy's coming!" That did it. They rushed

back in, looked around, looked
at each other, and waited for me
to speak.

I pointed to my lips and made
big wide words for them. "On the
dress-er! Be-hind you. Keys.
Keeeeeeeys. Get a chair, climb up,
get the keys, bring to Tommy."
They still looked blank. So I added,

"Tommy give you lollipop."

"Wollypocks!" they screamed …
and disappeared into the hall, going
"Nin-nah-nin-nah!" Seconds later,
they came back, staggering. They
were carrying Dad's laptop.

"Oh no!" I yelled. "Bad girls!
Daddy's! Precious! Not touch."

They dropped it as if it were red
hot. It made a
horribly loud
noise on the
stone floor.

KERRUNCH!

Help!

I couldn't BELIEVE it! Just when I thought Dad was getting back to normal, *bang* went his most precious thing!

I let my sticks drop. There was only one thing for it. Squeeze through the cat-flap myself. I was skinny enough, surely.

Heave. Hands in, arms in, head in – right up to my hips. The twins looked stunned. You'd look stunned if you saw me wiggling towards you like a big snake with its eyes popping out. Suddenly I stopped. My bum couldn't move forward – and it couldn't go back. I was STUCK! "Oh, heck!" I moaned.

The twins just sat with their thumbs in and blinked at me.

"Quick," I said, pointing at the keys on the hook on the dresser. "Get chair. Climb up. Bring keys to Tommy."

DING! That lit a light for Lottie. She ran out into the hall and staggered back in with the little oak table with the round top.

"No!" I screamed. "Don't climb on there, Lottie! That's antique! No! Use a chair!"

Too late. She shoved the table up against the dresser. Gemma helped her scramble on top of it. "Uppsa Daisy!" Then she climbed up on it, too. Lottie stood on tiptoe and reached for the keys.

That upset the balance. CRACK! all its legs slid out sideways. It was like watching a cow with all its hooves spreading out on a frozen pond. Very gently, almost in slow motion, the twins were lowered to the floor.

"AGAIN!" they yelled, but the table didn't want to play.

So Lottie ran over and put the keys in my mouth. I spat them out. "Put them in the lock!" I begged.

Then the phone rang. Gemma picked it up and looked at it.

"Hello! Is that Well Cottage?" said a loud high voice. "Guess who! I'm at the station!"

"Ding dong bell!" said Lottie.

"Tommy down da well," said Gemma into the phone.

"What?" said the voice.

"HELP!" I shouted.

"What's wrong with Tommy?" said the voice. "Surely he hasn't fallen down the well …?"

"Tissue! Tissue!" said Lottie.

"ALL FALL DOWN!" yelled Gemma into the phone.

"Help!" I yelled.

"My goodness! Now, don't panic!" said the voice. "Listen, listen! Where are Mummy and Daddy?"

"Over da hills and …" sang Lottie.

"FAR AWAY!" added Gemma noisily.

"Oh good gracious! Well, just hold on! Auntie's coming! I'll call the Fire Brigade! No I won't, no time. I'll jump in a taxi! Just hang on!"

Aunt Juniper to the Rescue

Aunt Juniper arrived in three minutes flat. Shame about the Fire Brigade, I'd like to have seen them. Maybe I would have got a look inside the fire engine.

"Mummy!" yelled the twins as she came charging round the back of the cottage. They could see her through the glass of the door.

Strong arms heaved me out of the cat-flap. I looked up and saw a very puzzled-looking taxi driver standing over me.

"Thank Heaven you're all right!" said Aunt Juniper. She knelt down right on the path and started covering my face with kisses. "Don't cry!"

OK, I *was* crying, but only because of Dad's laptop getting smashed. And I was too upset to explain. I passed her the keys and she unlocked the door and helped me get up on to my sticks. "Thank you, driver," she said, pushing a handful of money into his hand.

She stepped inside and cuddled the twins. I'd never seen them so quiet. They were puzzled. They put out their hands and touched her face. She looked like Mummy, she felt like Mummy, she smiled like Mummy, but there was something *different* about her.

"You are gorgeous!" said Aunt Juniper, examining them the way Mum and I used to look at the vase

she sent us. She turned to me.
"And so are you. Now, will you start explaining things first, or shall I?"

I started – by telling her about what happened after Mum and Dad set off with the chest. She started clearing up while she listened.
She sorted out the mess from the breakfast table. Somehow she even got the little round table back on its feet, so I said, "Hang on, Auntie."

I slid over to the kitchen cupboard on my bum. I said, "This has been put away for too long!"

And I got the vase out from under the sink (Phew!) and I stood it very, very carefully on the little round table. "There!" I said. "*That's* where it belongs."

"Thanks," she said. She seemed to understand that something important had just happened, so she just asked did I know when Mum and Dad would be back? I told her they wouldn't be long.

At that exact moment, I had the worst shock of my life. Mum and Dad threw open the front door.

Dark Time for Thomas Leo Falling! I panicked. I rushed to hide Dad's laptop under the sofa. But as I lunged forward, my stupid legs knocked the round table. It gave a shudder and down it went like a house of cards.

SMASH! went Aunt Juniper's vase on the hard stone floor.

Surprise!

Mum and Dad nearly jumped out of their skin.

"Oh my God!" Dad said. "Thomas! Are you all right?!!"

And then Mum said, "What did you say?"

And Dad said, "What?"

And Mum said, "Just now! You *SPOKE*, YOU BIG LUMMOCK! SO JUST DON'T STAND THERE, KISS ME!!!"

And Aunt Juniper said, "AND DON'T JUST STAND THERE KISSING EACH OTHER, KISS MEEEEE!!"
So there was loads of kissing and hugging and "What a fool I've been!" and "No, it was all my fault!" and "No, if only I'd listened" etc. etc.

I'm not going to go into everything that happened, just one thing. Dad said to Aunt Juniper what a big shame it was about her beautiful vase getting smashed before he could bring himself to look at it properly.

"Never mind," she said. "Now you'll have to look at me for a bit instead. Do you mind?"

He said no, he was really glad she'd come. He'd been trying for ages to say how DESPERATELY he wanted her to come. Only the words just wouldn't come out. "And the terrible thing is, I know how much that vase meant to June," he said.

"Yeah," said Mum. "Fifty-two thousand quid, at least."

"What!" said Dad. "You're kidding!"

"Nope," said Mum. "I looked it up online on your laptop. *An unusually large Wucai Beaker Vase. Gu Transitional Period. About 1650.* Right, Juniper?"

"Spot on!" said Aunt J.

I blushed. "Um, Dad," I began. "There's something you ought to know about your laptop."

Dad didn't hear me. He had his head in his hands and just kept repeating, "Fifty-two THOUSAND quid!"

Mum grinned. "So good thing I took the trouble to get it insured," she said.

Dad stretched out his arms. "I don't know what I've done to deserve this family!" he said.

Then everybody started talking
at once.

We didn't buy
another vase.
Dad mended
the old one.
And he mended
the round table
for it to go on.
Then he fixed

the sink and got cracking on the
rust on the Morris.

We spent some of the insurance
money on a people carrier and new
stuff for the twins.

I got an X-Box, but I still can't
work out if I deserved it. Oh, and
Dad got a new laptop.

He wrote and wrote, couldn't stop. He had so much to say. He reckons his latest book of poems is the best thing he's ever done.

The only thing he's stuck about is the title.

He's torn between *Mended, Finding the Key* and *Breaking the Silence*.

Mum likes *Falling Rising*, but I reckon *Through the Cat-Flap* is pretty good.

What do *you* think?